"Mom! Dad! The wing broke off my favorite airplane.
I need a new one." Said Lincoln.
Mom replied "Just play with your other airplanes."
"But this one was my favorite. Can I go shopping with
you today, please?" Lincoln pleaded

Mom took a pause, then said "You can come with me but we are not going to look at toys. Okay?"

At the store Lincoln sees a 747 aircraft, that glows in the dark.

"Mom look! This airplane looks even better than the one I had before and it glows in the dark."

"Not today" said mom. "If you wait a week maybe someone will buy it for your birthday."

Lincoln pressed his hand against the glass. "But they only have 2 left, and my birthday is a whole week away. They might be all sold out by then."

Mom had a list full of things to do. "We can talk about this later Lincoln. Its time to go."

At home Lincoln tells his dad all about the toy...

"...And" He added. "If you buy it today I'll act surprised when I open it on my birthday."

Dad laughed. "Well Lincoln it sounds like you thought this through. I'll tell you what.. if you continue to do all your chores and be a good boy, I'll take you shopping on your birthday. And I'll buy you whatever toy you want."

Lincoln quickly agreed by saying "Deal!"

That week Lincoln's behavior was more than good, it was great. He did all his chores with a smile.

He even tried to eat his vegetables.

On Friday morning while Lincoln was walking past the toy store he looked in the window and saw that there was only one airplane left. He thought to himself "If I wait until Saturday to go toy shopping, someone will buy the last airplane."

So he decided to take matters into his own hands. When no one was looking, Lincoln went into the store and stole the airplane.

At home Lincoln was so excited to play with his new toy that he immediately went into his room and played until the sun went down.

"Lincoln?! Time for dinner" mom yelled. When Lincoln heard his mom, he quickly hid the airplane under his mattress. He couldn't risk anyone finding out about the stolen toy.

At dinner mom and dad praised Lincoln for his great behavior that week. Dad said "We are so proud of you. Tomorrow morning I am going to take you to the store so you can pick out anything you want".

That night it was hard for Lincoln to sleep. He was overwhelmed with guilt. His parents were proud of him for being a "good kid" but deep down he knew that stealing was not a good thing to do.

The next morning when dad look Lincoln toy shopping, he didn't find anything in the store he wanted. Lincoln still felt guilty about stealing the toy yesterday. Dad said "Cheer up bud it's your birthday. How about I take you for ice cream?" Lincoln put his head down and said "I don't feel like getting ice cream can we just go home please?"

When Lincoln walked into the house, he walked into a

It was a surprise birthday party, with all of Lincolns friends. Lincoln and his friends had so much fun at the party, eating cake and playing games.

At the end of the party it was time to open presents.

Grandma and grandpa gave him $50 whole dollars.

To Lincoln,
Happy Birthday
-Love Grandma and Grandpa.

Finally Lincoln opened his present from mom and dad...

It was a glow in the dark 747 airplane!
Lincoln now had two of the same toy. He knew he had to
tell them the truth. So after everyone went home, he told
his parents about the toy he had been hiding.

Lincoln then took his parents in his room to show them the toy. As he lifted his mattress a piece fell to the floor. "Oh no!" Lincoln cried. "Its broken. I forgot it was under there last night and I slept on it."

Mom and dad had a talk with Lincoln.

Mom said "we appreciate you telling us the truth about the toy." Dad added "But, stealing is wrong and we need to do something to fix this."

So the next day Lincoln went back to the toy store and paid for the toy he stole. He used almost all of the money that grandma and grandpa gave him.

But he had just enough money left to get...

ICE CREAM!

Printed in Great Britain
by Amazon

19825332R00016